j398.2
G43K5

DETROIT PUBLIC LIBRARY

P9-EFJ-235

DETROIT PUBLIC LIBRARY
Chase Branch Library
17731 W. Seven Mile Rd.
Detroit, MI 48235
935-5346
DATE DUE

DEC 05 1994	
JAN 26 1995	JUL 1 7 1996
FEB 25 1995	AUG 1 9 1996
MAR 21 1995	
	MAR 1 8 1997
APR 22 1995	
JUN 1 2 1995	
	AUG 0 6 1997
AUG 0 2 1995	JAN 1 7 1998
NOV 25 1995	DEC 0 1 1998
JAN 0 3 1996	
FEB 1 2 1996	

BC-3

OCT 94

BASED ON A RUSSIAN TALE

THE KING WHO TRIED TO FRY AN EGG ON HIS HEAD

by Mirra Ginsburg
illustrated by Will Hillenbrand

MACMILLAN PUBLISHING COMPANY   NEW YORK

MAXWELL MACMILLAN CANADA   TORONTO

MAXWELL MACMILLAN INTERNATIONAL   NEW YORK   OXFORD   SINGAPORE   SYDNEY

A LONG, LONG TIME AGO, and far away, there lived a King. This King was very poor, and he was not very clever. He lived with his Queen and three beautiful daughters in a tumbledown palace. They had no servants, and no courtiers, and no soldiers, and no treasury. And often, when the peasants on their land forgot to bring them some bread, or meat, or carrots, they had to go without supper.

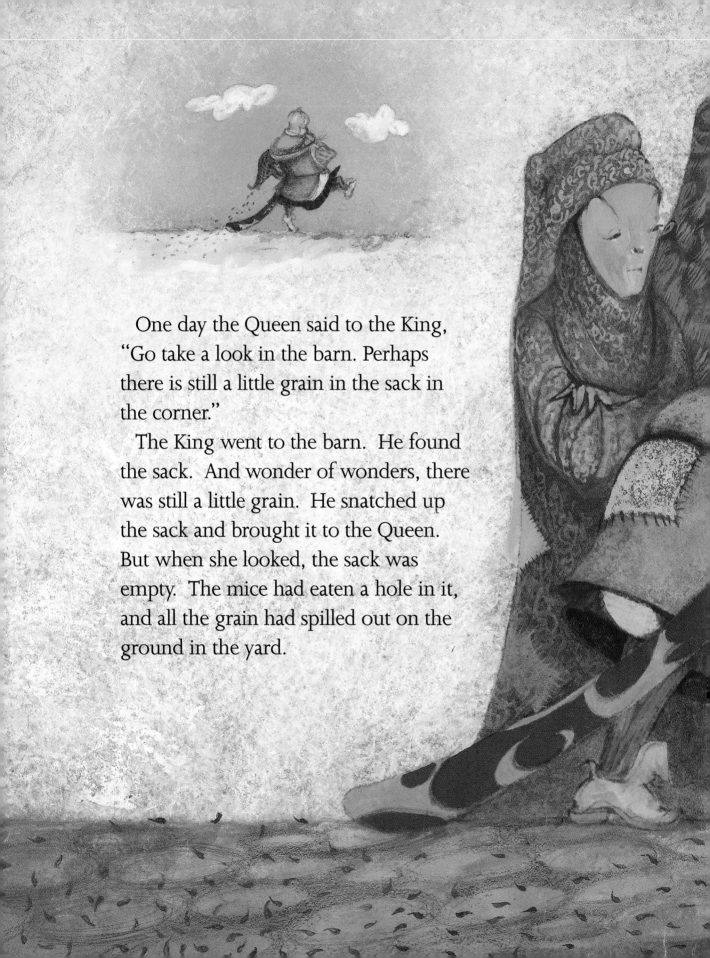

One day the Queen said to the King, "Go take a look in the barn. Perhaps there is still a little grain in the sack in the corner."

The King went to the barn. He found the sack. And wonder of wonders, there was still a little grain. He snatched up the sack and brought it to the Queen. But when she looked, the sack was empty. The mice had eaten a hole in it, and all the grain had spilled out on the ground in the yard.

"My unhappy wife!" cried the King. "And my unlucky daughters who must starve in my palace! No princes come to woo you because we are so poor."

They all sat down, and put their arms around each other, and wept.

Then the King went out into the yard and said, "If the Sun warms me, if the Moon gives me light, if the Raven helps me gather the grain I have spilled, I will let them marry my daughters."

The Sun warmed him, the Moon gave him
light, and the Raven helped him gather the grain
he had spilled.

The King and his family had kasha for supper.

The next morning, the
eldest princess went out on
the porch just as the Sun was rising. "What a lovely girl,"
cried the Sun. He swept her up and took her
to his golden house in the sky, and made her his wife.

In the evening, just as the
Moon appeared, the second
princess came out on the porch. "What a lovely girl,"
cried the Moon. He swept her up and took her
to his silver house in the sky, and made her his wife.

At night, when everything was dark, the youngest
princess came out on the porch. The great black Raven,
king of all the ravens, flew by and cried, "Oh, what a
lovely girl!" He swept her up and took her to his green
house in the woods, and made her his wife.

After a while, the King decided to visit his
daughters and see how they lived.

He went first to his eldest daughter in the Sun's
golden house. The princess and her husband
welcomed him, and in the morning the Sun said,
"Now I will make your breakfast." He sat down,
and broke an egg and poured it on his head. In a
minute, he served the King the tastiest omelette he
had ever eaten. After breakfast, the King went back
home to his Queen, laden with gold and presents,
and happy because his daughter lived so well.

"Come here, wife," he said when he got home. "Look at these lovely presents. We won't be poor from now on. And look at what I've learned from our clever son-in-law."

He told her to buy some eggs. "Now watch me," he said. "I will make you the tastiest omelette you have ever eaten."

He sat down, and he broke an egg, and poured it on his head. It trickled down his face and neck, and got into his collar. But "Wait," he said to his wife. "Just wait and see."

"I married a fool," she said. And she went to the stove and made herself the tastiest omelette she had ever eaten.

A week later the King went to visit his second daughter in the Moon's silver house. The princess and her husband welcomed him, and the Moon asked, "My dear father-in-law, what would you like for supper?"

"I am not hungry," said the King.

"Then how would you like a nice bath after your long journey?"

The Moon took him to the bathhouse and opened the door for him.

"But it is dark," the King said. "I'll trip and fall."

"Don't worry," said the Moon. He stuck his finger into a crack in the wall, and the bathhouse was lit up as by a dozen candles.

The next day the King
went back home to
his Queen, laden with
silver and presents, and
happy his daughter
lived so well.

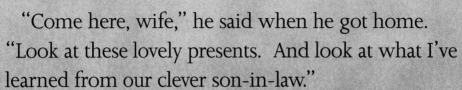

"Come here, wife," he said when he got home.
"Look at these lovely presents. And look at what I've
learned from our clever son-in-law."

By now it was evening, and he told his wife to heat
some water. Then took her to the bathhouse and said,
"Now you will take a nice warm bath."

"Who ever takes a bath at night?
It's dark in the bathhouse. I'll trip and fall."
   "Don't worry," said the King, and stuck his
finger into a crack in the wall. The bathhouse
remained as dark as it had always been at night.
But "Wait," he said to the Queen. "Just wait and see."
   "I married a fool," she said, and went back to the
        palace for her supper.

A week later the King went to visit his youngest daughter in the Raven's green house. The princess and her husband welcomed him. They talked and they laughed and made merry. When bedtime came, the Raven flew up on a branch and invited the King to join him. The old man puffed and huffed, but with his daughter's help he managed to climb up and settle next to the Raven. The Raven took him under his wing, and they slept safe and sound all night.

The next day the King set out for home, laden with presents and happy because all his daughters lived so well.

"Come here, wife," he said when he got home. "Look at these lovely presents. And later I will show you what I've learned from our clever son-in-law."

At bedtime, he led his wife out of the palace and into the garden. He chose a great old tree, and said to the Queen, "Now watch me, and do the same." He huffed and he puffed, and in the end he managed to climb up and settle on a branch. "Come up now, after me," he cried.

"I'm married to an old fool," said the Queen, and went back into the palace, to her nice soft warm bed.

But the King said, "I must practice what I've learned from my clever son-in-law."

He sat on the branch, and he got sleepier and sleepier.
At last he dozed off, and before he knew it, he came
tumbling down, all the way to the hard cold ground.

"Oh," he moaned, and "Never again," he groaned.
He limped off to the palace and quietly got into his
wife's nice soft warm bed. "Never again."

AND THEY LIVED PEACEFULLY

AND BY THEIR OWN WITS FOREVER AFTER.

For my parents with love
and my special friends at St. Joseph School
—W. H.

Text copyright © 1994 by Mirra Ginsburg
Illustration copyright © 1994 by Will Hillenbrand
All rights reserved. No part of this book may be reproduced or transmitted in any form or by any means, electronic
or mechanical, including photocopying, recording, or by any information storage and retrieval system, without
permission in writing from the Publisher. Macmillan Publishing Company is part of the Maxwell Communication Group
of Companies. Macmillan Publishing Company, 866 Third Avenue, New York, NY 10022. Maxwell Macmillan Canada,
Inc., 1200 Eglinton Avenue East, Suite 200, Don Mills, Ontario M3C 3N1. First edition. Printed in the United States of
America. The text of this book is set in 18 pt. Joanna. The illustrations are rendered in oil and oil pastel on paper.
10 9 8 7 6 5 4 3 2 1

Library of Congress Cataloging-in-Publication Data. Ginsburg, Mirra. The king who tried to fry an egg on
his head / by Mirra Ginsburg; illustrated by Will Hillenbrand. — 1st ed. p. cm. Summary: A poor and
foolish king marries off his three daughters to the Sun, the Moon, and the Raven, and then tries to copy
their special talents. ISBN 0-02-736242-6 [1. Folklore—Soviet Union.] I.Hillenbrand, Will, ill. II. Title.
PZ8.1.G455Ki 1994 398.2—dc20 [E] 91-10099

For my parents with love
and my special friends at St. Joseph School
—W. H.

Text copyright © 1994 by Mirra Ginsburg
Illustration copyright © 1994 by Will Hillenbrand
All rights reserved. No part of this book may be reproduced or transmitted in any form or by any means, electronic
or mechanical, including photocopying, recording, or by any information storage and retrieval system, without
permission in writing from the Publisher. Macmillan Publishing Company is part of the Maxwell Communication Group
of Companies. Macmillan Publishing Company, 866 Third Avenue, New York, NY 10022. Maxwell Macmillan Canada,
Inc., 1200 Eglinton Avenue East, Suite 200, Don Mills, Ontario M3C 3N1. First edition. Printed in the United States of
America. The text of this book is set in 18 pt. Joanna. The illustrations are rendered in oil and oil pastel on paper.
10 9 8 7 6 5 4 3 2 1

Library of Congress Cataloging-in-Publication Data. Ginsburg, Mirra. The king who tried to fry an egg on
his head / by Mirra Ginsburg; illustrated by Will Hillenbrand. — 1st ed.   p.   cm. Summary: A poor and
foolish king marries off his three daughters to the Sun, the Moon, and the Raven, and then tries to copy
their special talents. ISBN 0-02-736242-6 [1. Folklore—Soviet Union.] I. Hillenbrand, Will, ill. II. Title.
PZ8.1.G455Ki 1994 398.2—dc20 [E] 91-10099

He sat on the branch, and he got sleepier and sleepier. At last he dozed off, and before he knew it, he came tumbling down, all the way to the hard cold ground.

"Oh," he moaned, and "Never again," he groaned. He limped off to the palace and quietly got into his wife's nice soft warm bed. "Never again."

AND THEY LIVED PEACEFULLY
AND BY THEIR OWN WITS FOREVER AFTER.